What I did on my holiday

Alan Durant has written over a hundred books for children and young adults – and many more poems and stories. Some of his books have been shown on TV and he's won a few prizes, including The Royal Mail Scottish Children's Book Award. His books include *Burger Boy, Dear Father Christmas, Always and Forever, Football Fever, Game Boy* and *Poems from the Writing Shed.*

He frequently visits primary and secondary schools across the UK and abroad to encourage and inspire reading and writing. Many of the poems and stories in this book were themselves inspired by children (and adults) he's met along the way. Maybe after reading these poems and (very) short stories you'll have a go at writing your own. Or maybe you'll just go outside and kick a ball – as Alan would have done at your age. The main thing is to have fun!

I dedicate this book to all the children and teachers I've met in schools over the years, who've provided much of the inspiration for this book – and to Sam who made it come to life.

Copyright © Alan Durant 2016
Illustrations copyright © Samantha van Riet 2016
Designed by PixelPing Design
Published by Caboodle Books Ltd 2016

All rights reserved. Apart from any use permitted under UK copyright law, this publication may only be reproduced, stored or transmitted, in any form, or by any means, with prior permission in writing from the publishers or in the case of reprographic production, in accordance with the terms of licences issued by the Copyright Licensing Agency, and may not be otherwise circulated in any form of binding or cover other than that in which it is published and without a similar condition being imposed on the subsequent purchaser.

A Catalogue record for this book is available from the British Library.

ISBN: 9780995488502

Printed and bound by CPI Group (UK) Ltd, Croydon, CR0 4YY
The paper and board used in this book are natural recyclable products made from wood grown in sustainable forests. The manufacturing processes conform to the environmental regulations of the country of origin.

CABOODLE BOOKS LTD
Riversdale
8 Rivock Avenue
Steeton
BD20 6SA
UK

www.authorsabroad.com
www.alandurant.co.uk
www.samvanriet.co.za
www.pixelpingdesign.co.za

What I did on my holiday

Alan Durant

Illustrated by Sam van Riet

CABOODLE BOOKS LTD

Contents

What I Did On My Holiday 6
Billy Wiggins 7
Spring Cleaning 8
Ping Pong 9
A Boy Kicking a Ball Against a Wall 10
Snakes 11
A Special Visitor 12
A Day at the Seaside 14
The Friendship Tree 16
Apple 17
Orange 17
The Thought-Football 18
Stroke the Cat 20
Can I Stay Up Late Tonight? 22
Coco Discovers the World 24
Aerobatics 25
Puja in the Bathroom 26
Copycat 28
The Gorgon's Curse 29
A Close Shave 30
The First Day 32
Skyline Sequence 34
Fireworks' Night 37
Spoilt for Choice 38
Bags of Inspiration 40
Rósín Builds a Mountain 42

Spring Has Sprung!	43
What's Science?	44
A Mystery Solved	46
A Brush with Danger	48
Tommy-All-Alone	51
The Science Lesson	52
We Writers	54
Idiot Acrostic	55
Standing on Ceremony	56
Three Library Acrostics	57
Time Flies	58
Pink	60
African Animal Conundrum	61
The Dog Who Cried "Custard!"	62
Three Wishes	64
Trick or Treat	66
The Moment After	68
Valentine's Poem	69
Catastrophe	70
Have You Ever Contemplated?	72
The Dream	73
If I Won the Lottery	74
Moving	76
Noughts and Crosses	77
Home At Last	78
Crossing the Bridge	80

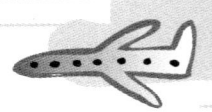

What I Did On My Holiday

This year on my holiday I went to the toilet one hundred and forty-two times. This is an estimate not an exact figure, because I did not keep a record. I worked this figure out by multiplying the number of days of my holiday by the average number of times I went to the toilet each day. This year we had forty five days of holiday and I went to the toilet three times each day on average. Three times forty-five is one hundred and thirty-five. That leaves a difference of seven. But I can explain.

On one day on my holiday I had diarrhoea. The day I had diarrhoea I went to the toilet ten times – approximately. I went like the clappers. That is a simile. I do not know what clappers are but to go like them means to go very fast. I did go very fast that day and so did the diarrhoea. It went down the toilet like the clappers. You could say it went like the crappers. That is a pun on the name Thomas Crapper. Thomas Crapper was the man who invented the flushing toilet. Some people think he invented the toilet, but he didn't – he invented the flush. So when you go to the toilet, you flush like the Crappers.

This year on my holiday I also went to Disneyland in Florida. I flew on a plane. On the plane I went to the toilet. When you lock the toilet door the light comes on. When you unlock the toilet door the light goes off. I can't wait for my next holiday to go flying again.

Billy Wiggins

A boy named Billy Wiggins lives in his school.
At night in the darkness he creeps into the hall.
He sits on the floor, waiting for the other children to arrive.
But there's no assembly at midnight – and Billy's not alive.

He prowls the empty classrooms and corridors,
Recalling regretfully displays of poetry, maths and art.
He peers in cupboards, hoping laughter will tumble out,
But the blistered dark can't raise the spirits of Billy's
ghostly heart.

He slips beneath the locked front door,
Glides out into the foot-scuffed charcoal playground.
But where once he joined in noisy games of tag,
Now all's slate silent; there's not a sound.

It's lonely being a ghost without a single friend,
Doomed to roam a cheerless school for ever without end.
The deed he did haunts him, brands him death's sad fool,
He wishes he could change that night
Billy burnt down the school.

Spring Cleaning
An Interactive Rhyme

Sweep sweep sweep the house
Scrub scrub scrub the floor
Shine shine shine the glass
Paint paint paint the door.

Shake shake shake the rug
Dust dust dust the room
Polish polish polish the wood
Sweep sweep sweep the broom

Scrub scrub scrub the dog
Dust dust dust the cat
Shake shake shake your head
Polish polish polish your hat

Shine shine shine the sun
Dust dust dust your ma
Scrub scrub scrub your ears
Paint paint paint the car

Polish polish polish the bread
Shake shake shake the chair
Sweep sweep sweep the bed
Dust dust dust your hair

Paint paint paint your pants
Scrub scrub scrub the king
Polish polish polish the sky
And that's the way to clean the Spring!

Ping Pong

See the ball bounce on the table,
Back and forth across the net,
Spinning like a month of Sundays,
Powered by a turbo jet.

Side spin, back spin,
Front spin, top spin,
Whirling, twirling,
Twisting, turning.

Faster than a speeding bullet,
Faster than an express train,
Faster than a shooting comet,
Faster than a fighter plane.

Faster than a dash of cheetahs,
Faster than a scratch of fleas,
Faster than a flash of lightning,
Faster than the wildest sneeze.

Faster than the hand can scribble,
Faster than the eye can blink,
Faster than the tongue can babble,
Faster than the mind can

                think.

A Boy Kicking a Ball Against a Wall

P-top p-top!
P-top p-top!
P-top p-top!
In the cool of an early Spring morning
in Cape Town
a boy kicks a ball against a wall.
P-top p-top!
P-top p-top!
From foot to wall to ground,
foot to wall to ground.

The sound echoes through
the cloud-blotted sky
from the concrete city
to a leafy suburb
over fields and vineyards
to a wood and corrugated-iron
shanty town,
where a boy kicks a ball against a wall.
P-top p-top!
P-top p-top!
A boy kicking a ball against a wall,
      kicking a ball against a wall,
            against a wall.

Snakes

Miss Kaye, my Reception teacher,
promised a prize to anyone
who could tie their shoelaces.
I wanted that prize.
It was a little blue notebook
with a little blue pencil.
But I couldn't tie my laces.
I tried, how I tried,
but the laces were snakes
beneath my fingers, slithering
away when I tried to loop them,
escaping my knots and
flattening out again.

So I cheated.
I took off my shoes,
and when no one was looking,
I slipped them on again with the laces
already done up. "Look, Miss,"
I beamed, "I tied my laces."
Miss Kaye smiled. "Well done,
you clever boy," she said.
She gave me a little blue notebook
and a little blue pencil.
I opened up the book and wrote my name.
And every letter burned with shame.

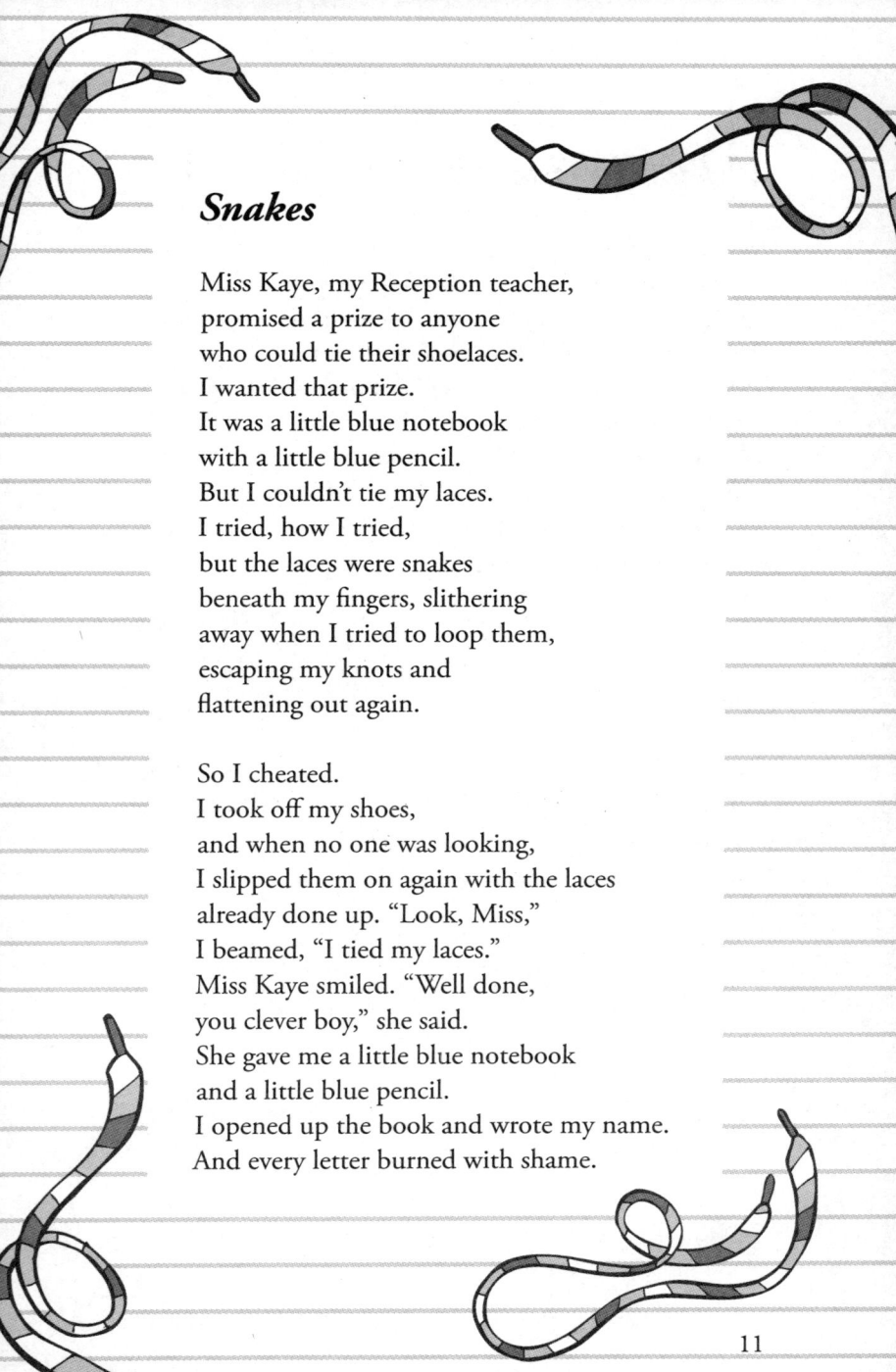

A Special Visitor

The day the famous writer came to visit our school, everyone was very excited. Mr Holland, our teacher, wore his best tie. "I don't want anyone asking any stupid questions," he said, "like what is your favourite colour or how much do you earn or what is your fourth longest book. Is that understood?"

"Yes, sir," the class replied.

I put up my hand. "And, Joshua," Mr Holland said, "I especially don't want to hear any of your weird stuff. In fact I'd rather you said nothing at all."

"Yes, sir," I muttered.

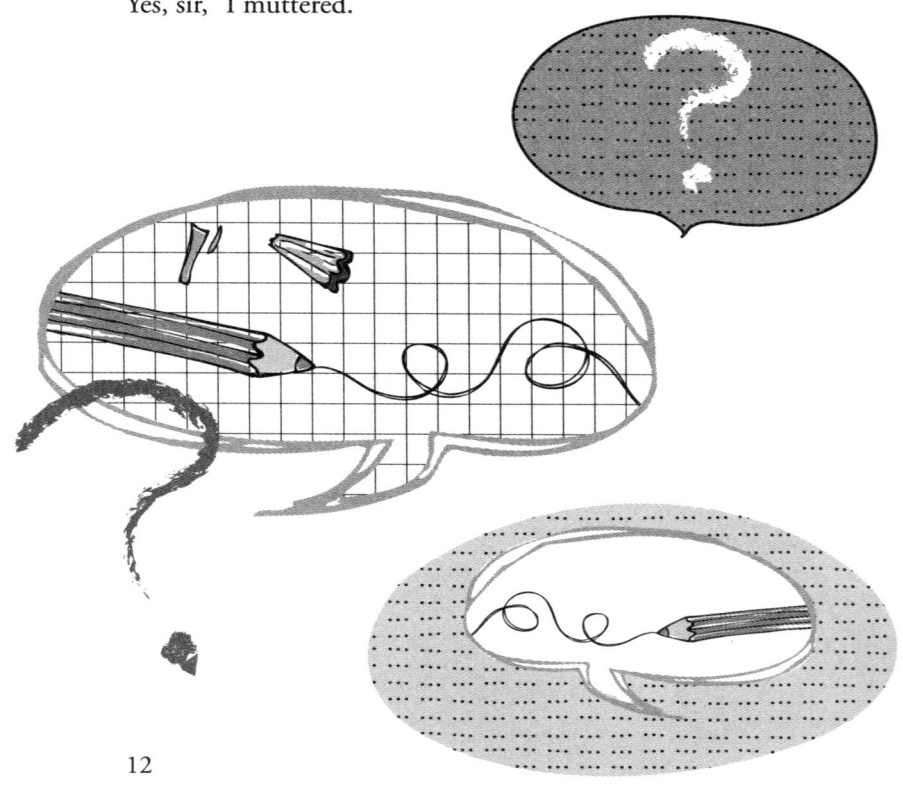

As it happens, I did have a question I wanted to ask the famous writer. I wanted to ask him if he wrote with a pencil and did it matter if the pencil was sharp or blunt. When you see the print on the page and it's black and clear do you feel differently from when it's a bit blurry, I would ask him. I do. I hate blunt pencils. My pencil must be sharp. Sometimes I sharpen my pencil twenty times because it keeps breaking and I have to have a proper point. I can't write a story unless my pencil point is sharp. That's what I was going to tell the famous writer and see if he felt the same.

But I never asked the famous writer my question because Mr Holland told me not to. He answered lots of questions about his stories and where his ideas came from and all the different countries that his books were sold in. He told us about the shed he worked in and how many words he wrote each day. But whether he used a pencil or not and, if so, whether it had to be sharp, nobody asked and he didn't say.

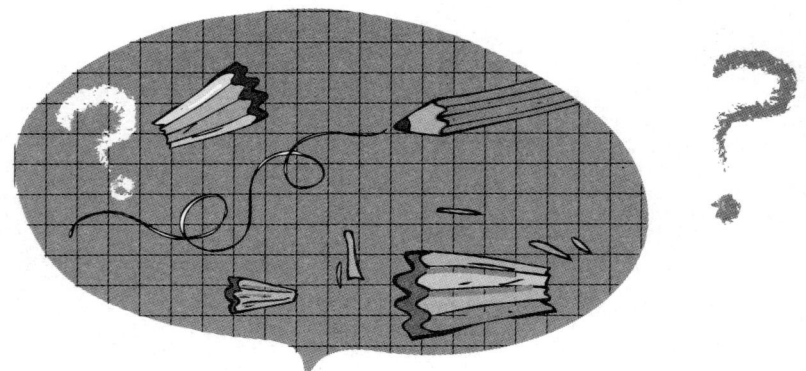

A Day at the Seaside

I was floating on Dad's last breath. I didn't know it then of course. If I'd known what was going to happen I'd never have asked him to blow up the stupid lilo.

I saw it in a tacky beach shop. There were buckets, spades, flags, balls and inflatables of all shapes and sizes. This one was bright pink with yellow flowers. I wanted it as soon as I saw it. Dad was happy to buy it for me too. I guess he thought it would make our day at the seaside less stressful. I'd spend the day playing in the water and he'd sit in his deckchair and read the paper. We'd both be happy.

He didn't even moan really about blowing the thing up. It was a hot day and it took him ages. His face was scarlet. He blew out his cheeks like one of those old jazz trumpeters and slowly the thing bulked up. He paused and panted for a bit and joked that he was too old for this sort of thing and we both laughed. He wasn't old and he was very fit. He went to the gym most days.

That's why I couldn't believe it when it happened. I'd hardly been in the sea for any time when I heard the shouting on the beach. Dad was lying face down in the sand. I rolled off the lilo and ran through the waves to the shore.

He'd had a massive heart attack the medics told me later when they'd tried but failed to revive him. He'd probably died instantaneously. I looked disbelievingly at his lifeless body. There was no breath left in him. It was all in that lilo, that horrible pink lilo, drifting away out to sea…

The Friendship Tree

The Friendship Tree
has twenty-three
rectangular, plastic leaves
of red and blue and green
attached with string
to the branches happily
by the children of Year 3
with messages of friendship.

Yet some have fallen.

Is it because Chloe wouldn't let Jacob
join in with her skipping game?
Or Ryan told tales on Ben?
Or because Morgan and Rachel
called each other names?
Or because one day Cody
refused to sit next to Kai?

Or was it the bully wind,
kicking and cursing,
tugging and taunting
angry that no one,
not even the gorgeous, ever popular sun
would be *his* friend?

Apple

Apple crumble, apple tart
Baked in the oven with sugar and spice,
Apple fritters, apple sauce,
On our plates you look so nice.
We peel you, slice you,
Stew you, mash you,
We serve you up in a pie.
But it's on the tree,
So handsome in your red and green,
That you're truly the apple of our eye.

Orange

Your pitted skin's appealing,
I'm sure we'd all agree,
Inside you're sweet and juicy
And rich in vitamin C,
Your scent is most enticing
I long for you on my lips,
But there's just one problem with you,
That's your pith and pips!

The Thought-Football

Today's literacy task is to write a poem.
I've written one line:
the date and the learning objective.
The learning objective is to write a poem.
My page is blank. My mind is blank.
I can't do poems.
I never know what to write.

Yesterday our teacher, Miss Walsh,
read us a poem by a famous poet.
Ted something. (I don't remember his other name.)
The poem was called The Thought-Fox.
It was about the poet sitting at his desk with a blank page,
not knowing what to write,
when a fox appears outside his window
and he writes a poem about that.

I am looking out the window.
I can see Mr Brown, the caretaker.
He is sweeping up leaves.
Now he is gobbing on the grass.
I can't write about that.
Maybe I should write about
the weather: it's horrible.
The sky is grey, the colour of boring,
the colour of wet play.
I don't want to write about that.

I'm stuck.
Stuckstuckstusckstuckstuck.

I wish a fox would appear
or better still a football,
bobbing about on the playground.
I'm good at football.
I know what to do with the ball.
I'd run out and kick it.
Then I'd flick it in the air
and do keepy-uppies.
I'd try to beat my record (137).
Then I'd play a match with my friends.
I'd score loads of goals like I always do.
And we'd shout a lot.
And we'd laugh a lot too.

But now it's starting to rain.
So there won't be no football today.
We'll have to stay inside and finish our work.
Finish our poems.

How am I going to do that
when I don't even know how to start?

Stroke the Cat
An Interactive Rhyme

Stroke the cat, stroke the cat,
Feel her fur
Storke the cat, stroke the cat,
Hear her purr.
Stroke her like that.
Don't stroke her like this.
If you stroke her like this
She'll scratch and hiss.
Sssssss!

Pat the dog, pat the dog,
Shake his paw.
Pat the dog, pat the dog,
He'll roll on the floor.
You can tickle his tummy,
But don't pull his tail.
If you pull his tail,
He'll bite and yell.
Hoooowl!

Ride the horse, ride the horse,
Ruffle his mane.
Ride the horse, ride the horse,
Feed him some grain.
Hold the reins steady,
Don't let the reins go slack.
If you let the reins go slack,
Then he'll toss you off his back.
Neigh!

Rock the babe, rock the babe,
Sing a lullaby.
Rock the babe, rock the babe,
Hear her sweetly sigh, aaahhh.
Rock the baby gently,
But don't let the baby fall.
If you let the baby fall
Oh my how she'll bawl.
Waaaaa!

Can I Stay Up Late Tonight?

Jamie: Mum, can I stay up late tonight?
There's a film I want to watch on TV.
Mum: What film?
Jamie: It's called Return of the Blood-sucking Zombies.
Mum: No, you can't watch that. It isn't suitable.
Jamie: Why not?
Mum: Because it isn't for children your age.
Jamie: Why not?
Mum: Because it's violent and nasty and very scary.
Jamie: I know, that's why I want to watch it.
Mum: It will give you nightmares.
Jamie: I don't get nightmares.
Mum: You will if you watch that film.
Jamie: All my friends are going to watch it.
Mum: Well, their parents shouldn't let them.
It has a 15 certificate.
Jamie: But they'll all be talking about it tomorrow at school and I'll feel stupid because I wasn't allowed to watch it.

Mum: Jamie, I'm not going to allow you to watch Return of the Blood-sucking Zombies and that is that. It isn't suitable and it's on much too late.
Jamie: It's not fair!
Mum: Yes it is. It's not only fair, it's right.
Jamie: I hate you!
Mum: Don't be silly, Jamie, or I'll send you to bed right now.
Jamie: I may as well go to bed. There's nothing good on TV.
Mum: Look, I'll tell you what. I'll get a DVD out tomorrow – something we can watch together.
Jamie: Like what?
Mum: Like … Bambi.
Jamie: Bambi! I'm not watching that. It'll give me nightmares!

Coco Discovers the World

A hamster's life is short
and not so very interesting;
Coco nestles down in the straw
of his oblong prison,
and, at night, relieves the boredom
by climbing aboard the wheel
and spinning himself dizzy.
Now and then he finds himself lifted
in the furless cradle of a human hand
or pouched in a pocket like a baby marsupial.

But, suddenly one day,
his marginalised world expands extraordinarily.
He whirls about the house
in a transparent perspex bowl,
moving through dark and light,
exploring new vistas,
revolving along a sea of corridors,
continents blurring around him.
He is a diver in a diving bowl.
He is an astronaut in a space capsule.
He is the Earth orbiting the Sun.

Round and round, over and over,
Coco rolls, Coco rocks!
If he were human, he would raise a flag;
but he's a rodent.
At the height of his glory,
the cat intercepts him,
flicks open the bowl,
and bites off his exhilarated head.

Aerobatics
(a haiku)

Over these hill fields
The silent kite glides and wheels
Practising his skills.

Puja in the Bathroom

This week we had a visit from an author.
He told us lots of things about his life.
One thing he told us was that when he was a child like us
he used to sit in the toilet and make up stories.
He made up stories to fit the pictures he saw in the patterns
in the toilet's lino floor.
Sometimes, in the toilet, he talked to his imaginary
　friend too.
She was called Dee Dee.

I don't have an imaginary friend.
But sometimes I lock myself in the bathroom
and I talk to myself in the mirror.
Sometimes we argue, myself and I.
Sometimes we shout at each other.
"Shut up, you!" I shout and I wag my finger.
"Shut up, you!" shouts me-in-the-mirror,
wagging her finger back.
"No, you shut up!" I say.
"No, you shut up," says me-in-the-mirror.
Then I stick out my tongue
and me-in-the-mirror does the same.

Sometimes I don't talk to the mirror;
my hands talk instead.

I pretend my fingers are a family:
my little finger is a child,
the next one is a mummy,
the middle one is a daddy,
then there's a grandpa
and my thumb is a grandma.
And my other hand is a family too.

Sometimes the two families have a conversation.
The children talk to each other about school.
The grandmas and grandpas talk to each other about the
   old days.
The fathers have a boring conversation about cricket or cars.
Sometimes the mummies talk about their children.
They say things like, "Did you know there has been
an author visiting the school this week?
Apparently he's been sitting in the toilet all day
talking to himself and making up stories."
And then they shake their heads and tut.
"The things they teach in schools these days," they say.

Then my brother knocks on the bathroom door
and shouts: "Get out of that bathroom right now, Puja!
I've got to have a pee!"

Copycat

Hello.
Hello.
How are you?
How are you?
I'm very well thanks.
I'm very well thanks.
Good.
Good.

Why are you copying everything I say?
Why are you copying everything I say?
I'm not.
I'm not.
Yes you are.
Yes you are.
It's really annoying.
It's really annoying.
You're stupid.
You're stupid.

Ok.
Ok.
I'm a great big ugly, bug-eyed, buck-toothed,
elephant-eared, fat-faced, hairy-toed idiot.
You're a great big ugly, bug-eyed, buck-toothed, elephant-eared, fat-faced, hairy-toed idiot.
That's not fair, you didn't copy me.
Why would I want to copy an idiot?

The Gorgon's Curse

I, Medusa, the Gorgon,
sister of Sthermo and Euryale,
curse you, Perseus, and all your brood
ever until eternity.

May snakes nest and coil in your hair
And seep your brain with poison.
May your eyes see only ugliness,
Your ears hear only turmoil.
May your nose be filled with the stench of your own
   flesh rotting.
May your teeth crumble and turn to dust in your mouth.
May your lips suppurate with sores.
May boils and carbuncles blight your cheeks.

May your heart be forever tortured by the Sirens' song.
May your liver be devoured daily by Harpies.
May your spleen be savaged by Cerebrus, the
   three-headed dog.
May your kidneys be the Scylla's sweetmeats.
May the chimera's fiery breath boil your blood to madness.

May you be turned to stone.

I, Medusa, curse you!

A Close Shave

The Man sat back in the chair and closed his eyes.
"What is that delicious smell?" he murmured.
"Ah, that'll be the pies," the barber chuckled, "in my wife's shop next door."
"I could die for one of those," sighed the man.
"Aye," nodded the barber, "I'm sure you could, sir – and you wouldn't be the first."
He dragged the cutthroat razor expertly through the foam that covered the man's chin. Then he rinsed it in the waiting bowl of hot water, before starting on the man's cheeks.

"I see in the papers that another local man's gone missing," the man said, "That makes eight now – and no sign of a body."
"Perhaps it's something in the air," the barber suggested.
"Well, it's a mystery all right," the man agreed.

The barber carefully scraped away the stubble from the man's upper lip.
"Were any of them customers of yours?" the man asked, running his hand appreciatively over his smooth, unmarked skin.
"Well, yes, sir, they were actually," the barber said, "all of them."
"Well, fancy that," said the man with a shake of his head.

The barber brushed a soapy froth across the man's neck. As he lifted the razor, he smiled strangely and there was a gleam of wild excitement in his eyes. He put the blade against the man's jugular vein. His grip tightened, preparing to cut ... when the shop bell rang and a lad burst in.

"Quick, Bert! The boss says you're to come at once!"

The man was already on his feet and rubbing a towel across his neck. He took a note from his wallet and handed it to the barber.

"Sorry, Sweeney," he said, smiling, "you'll have to save my neck for next time."

The First Day

First Days were always the worst, starting out at a new place, being the newcomer. As he came through the gates he took in the scene. It was the usual mixture of boisterous activity – running, chasing, jumping, screeching – and silent staring. He hated those stares: some curious, some friendly, some searching you out, looking for signs of weakness. There was one in the middle, fixing him with a tough, challenging stare. He'd have to watch out for him. It wouldn't be long before they'd come to blows. When the time came, he'd expect the newcomer to back down, roll over, but this newcomer never did. That was "the problem".

"Disruptive and anti-social" they'd called him at the last place, before kicking him out. And it wasn't the first time. But that was the way it was, the law of the jungle. He wasn't going to be meek and mild just to fit in. If that was the lesson they wanted to teach him, well, they could forget it. He wasn't into lessons anyway. What they hadn't understood – no one had – was that he didn't want to be in a place like this. He felt cooped up, trapped, stifled. He wanted to be free, his own master, doing whatever he pleased.

The door opened and his minder pushed him in so that he fell on all fours.

"Watch out for that one, he bites," the man warned no one in particular.

Yes, he thought, bites – and scratches and kicks too. I'm a nasty piece of work I am. He looked up and took a stance that he hoped was intimidating.

The door clanged shut behind him.

"Crazy chimp," said the keeper. "He's worse than us."

Skyline Sequence

Sunrise

Come, sun.
Can't you hear the birds whistle?
Don't you know it's day?

Run, sun, up and down the brown houses
into the green trees,
over the purple white-edged hills,
by the blue seas.
Wake the world!
It's time to have fun!

Clouds

Above the long, gray line of roof tops
the sky is shining cats and dogs,
sheep and badgers, hares and bears,
and I think I saw an icy white dinosaur.

Top of the Pots
See the seagulls
on top of the pots
on the chimney stacks
like Lego bricks.

A gull rises,
its white wings open out
like the pages of a book.
It writes its flight across the sky.

Mountains
The mountains are huge triangles of rock.
They zig zag across the clear blue sky,
their icy tips touch the edges of the curved clouds,
but the hot sun melts them and they cry.

Pagoda Palace 
We are the king and queen,
our palace is made of sweets,
red, gold and green,
with wafers of rich chocolate
and an upside down
ice-cream.

The Kite and the Moon

Above the pale round domes
the purple kite, a boy's toy,
dodges and twitches.

It thinks the moon is a balloon.
"Let's make friends!" it shouts
"We can dance and play.
Then, you and me, we'll fly away!"

Towers

The pin tops of the towers
are so high
they are out of this world.
Huge as rockets
they gleam and glow
in the black night
as if they came back from space
stuck with stars.

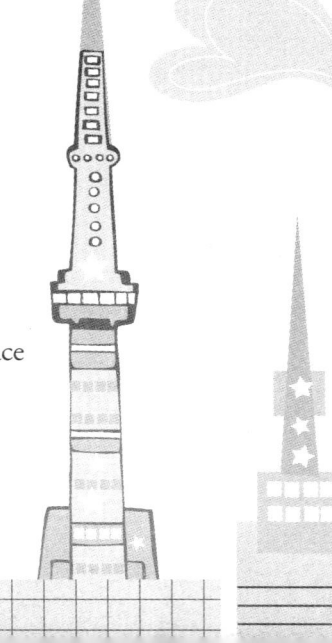

Fireworks' Night

Who'd be a cat on Fireworks' Night,
When whizz-bang rockets crack the sky
And sudden booms blast the night?
Who'd be a cat? Not I.

Who'd be a bird on Fireworks' Night,
Sparks singeing feathers as they fly,
And the calm clear air all thunder and smoke?
Who'd be a bird? Not I.

Who'd be a guy on Fireworks' Night,
On top of a pyre as the flames leap high,
Burned to ashes while children cheer?
Who'd be a guy? Not I.

Who'd be a child on Fireworks' Night,
As Catherine wheels spin on the tree
And the dark world sears in colour and bang?
Who'd be a child on that night? Me!

Spoilt for Choice

One fine evening my mother said to me,
"My dear darling Alan, what would you like for tea?
Maybe fish and chips or hot pot?
Spaghetti or macaroni cheese?
Eggs on toast with vinegar?
Sausages with gravy and mushy peas?
Roast lamb with mashed potatoes?
Stir fry or spicy chicken curry?
A burger with salad and French fries?
A pizza with slices of pepperoni?
Duck a l'orange, my sweet one?
Steak tartare or cassoulet?
Tasty snails in garlic butter?
Boeuf Bourguignon or jambon fricassee?
My dear darling Alan, tell me,
What would you like for tea?"
And I said, "Jelly."

"Jelly, my dear darling Alan," my mother said to me.
"If jelly it is you really want, then jelly it shall be.
Would you like strawberry jelly or raspberry?
Lemon or lime, orange or gooseberry?
Red jelly, yellow jelly, jelly that's pink or gold?
Jelly shaped like a rabbit from my special jelly mould?
Jelly that wibbles and wobbles, jelly that stands up tall?
Jelly that melts in your mouth, jelly that's warm or cool?
Milk jelly, chocolate jelly, jelly from the deli?
Jelly that's so sweet, it will sing in your belly?
Tell me my dear darling Alan, please tell me, do,
What kind of jelly shall I make for you?"
And I said, "Blue."

"Blue jelly, my dear darling Alan," my mother said to me,
"If blue jelly's what you want, blue jelly it shall be.
I'll make you delicious blue jelly for your tea.
Would you like baby blue or turquoise, royal blue or navy?
The blue of a clear, bright sky or a sea all wild and wavy?
Cyan or aquamarine, midnight blue or duck egg?
Blue like the jeans you wear or the
  veins running down your leg?
Azure blue or cobalt, air force blue or peacock?
Blue as lapis lazuli or an early summer forget-me-not?
Blue like when you're feeling sad?
Or the spots of mould on food that's bad?
Blue as cornflowers in a field, blue as sparkling sapphires?
Blue as your fingers in the cold or blue as gas-flame fires?
"My dear darling Alan, tell me," my mother said to me,
"What shade of blue jelly would you like for your tea?"
And I said, "Actually, Mum, I think I'll just have a salad."

Bags of Inspiration

There was once a boy who was set a task by his teacher. This task was to write a story – and not an ordinary or dull story but a story that would make the teacher sit up in her chair and shout "Wow!" Now this was a very difficult task for the boy because he was not the best storyteller in his class and he had no idea what to write about. His gran, however, was great at making up stories. So the boy phoned his gran and asked if she could help him – and she said that she could.

"I'll send you bags of inspiration," she said.

"Oh," said the boy, a little disappointed, because he had hoped for more than his gran's good wishes.

The next morning there was a knock on the front door. The boy opened it.

"I have a delivery for you," said the postman. He brought out three bags from his van.

"What's that?" asked the boy.

"Inspiration," said the postman. "Well, that's what it says on the bags."

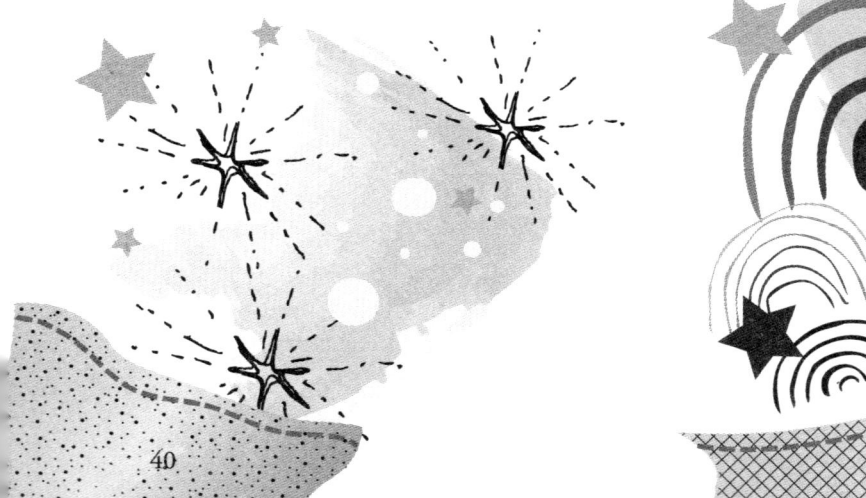

Puzzled, the boy took the bags into the house and opened them one by one. In the first bag he found light so warm and bright that it made his face glow. In the second was a riotous rainbow of colours that turned his eyes to joyous kaleidoscopes. In the third bag, in the third bag, he found words and phrases – a flood of language that spilled out over his hands and filled him suddenly so full of inspiration he had to write. That very moment he sat down and wrote a story – not an ordinary or dull story, but a story that made his teacher sit up in her chair and shout "Wow!" And so will you too if, one day, he should read that story to you.

Róisín Builds a Mountain

It
starts
(as it so often does)
with a dictionary – small, concise,
yet plump with words and meanings,
quickly followed by a thesaurus, which,
the teacher opines, is packed with interesting
alternatives for common words such as "says", for
example, and this being Connemara in County Galway,
of course there must be a *foclóir* of the Irish language too.
Next comes a bible, plain and sturdy (and rarely referred to),
sitting atop the class reading book, a collection of traditional tales,
then the story that Róisín reads for her pleasure, the Big Friendly Giant,
beneath him the world expands yet more in the form of a full-colour atlas,
but even this is dwarfed by the fact-filled encyclopaedia of people and places,
which finds itself resting heavily upon the back of a science text about vertebrates,
the brunt of whose weight is taken by an illustrated history of the Second World War.
And still the mountain rises – with maths and spelling books, times tables, a homework diary,
Up and up and up it climbs towards the classroom ceiling, concealing Róisín entirely from view,
a mountain of knowledge, of learning, of wonder, every bit as glorious as the Connemara hills beyond.

Spring Has Sprung!

Spring has sprung!
Buds are popping,
bunnies are hopping,
there's no stopping
the Spring. It's sprung!

Spring has sprung!
The sap is rising,
the world's surprising,
there's no disguising
that Spring has sprung!

Spring has sprung!
The birds are singing,
the leaves are greening,
the soil has meaning,
coz Spring has sprung!

Spring has sprung!
Shrubs are sprouting
the sheep are shouting,
there's no doubting
that Spring has sprung!

Take a look around you,
it surely will astound you.
Yes, Spring has sprung.
Boing!

What's Science?

Magnesium, iron, copper and zinc,
turning sheets of litmus paper blue or pink,
mixing up chemicals to make a great big stink,
that's science!

Bunsen burners, test-tubes, glass bell jars,
satellite photos of Jupiter and Mars,
gazing through telescopes to understand the stars,
that's science!

Gases, liquids, CO2 and H2O,
studying life forms to see how they grow,
boiling up kettles and melting down snow,
that's science!

Motors, engines, reels and wheels that spin,
the role of muscles, organs, bones and skin,
people in lab coats experimenting,
that's science!

Rocks and fossils, chalk and clay and sand,
medicines, vitamins, machines that x-ray and scan,
a catapult made from a huge elastic band,
that's science!

Chemistry, physics and biology,
the birds in the sky and the fish in the sea,
the ozone layer and climatology,
that's science!

Life, death, everything – you and me,
that's science!

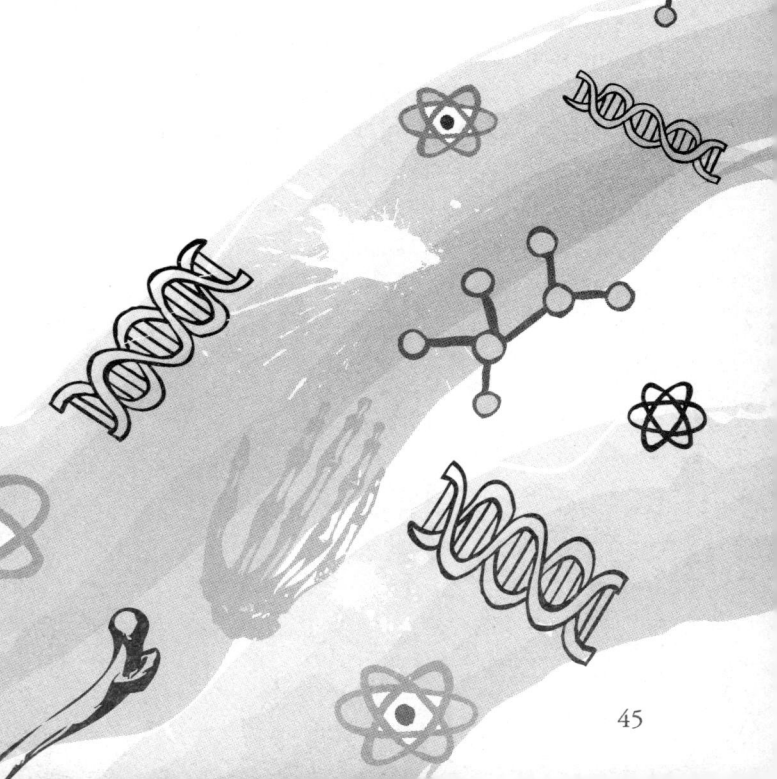

A Mystery Solved

Jed Burke was baffled. No, more than baffled, he was perplexed. For weeks now he had been plagued by an irritating problem: his socks kept disappearing. Where did they go? Was someone taking them?

Every time Jed put his socks in the wash one or two would vanish. He barely had a matching pair left in his drawer. When he mentioned it to his mum, she just shrugged. "It's just one of life's little mysteries," she said. But to Jed it was no longer little – and he wanted an answer.

Could it be that someone or something was stealing the socks off the washing line, he wondered. Determined to find out, he rigged up a CCTV camera in the garden. This will solve the mystery, he thought. It seemed a perfect plan, but when he looked through the footage later, all he saw was hours and hours of washing hanging on a line. It was as dull as, well, watching washing dry.

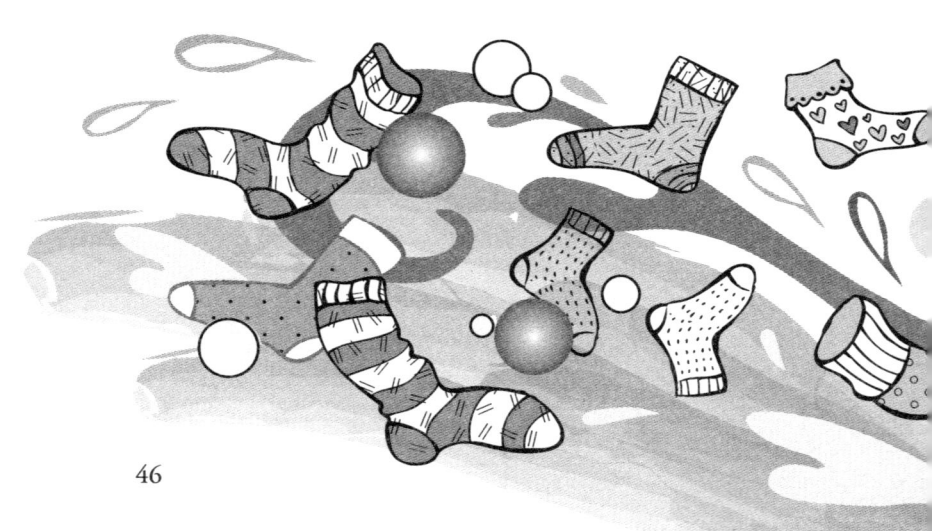

There was only one thing for it, he decided. The next time his mum put a wash on, Jed climbed into the washing machine, fully clothed, so that he wouldn't be noticed. Now at last he'd solve the mystery of the disappearing socks… And he did.

As the washing machine churned and juddered and span, Jed found the solution to the mystery that had baffled him for so long. He saw with his own eyes the machine gobble his socks with sly greed. Unfortunately for Jed, however, the machine also devoured him – socks, pants, t-shirt, head, the lot.

The disappearance of Jed Burke is a mystery that has never been solved.

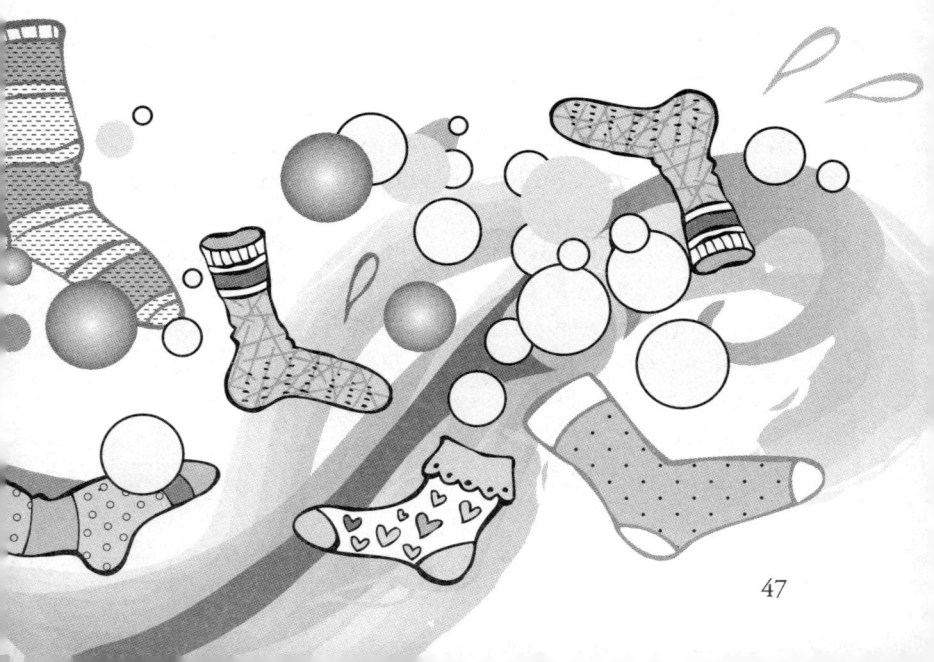

A Brush with Danger

I was brushing my teeth one night when blood started to gush from my gums. The toothpaste foam was no longer white but bright red. I couldn't believe it. I shut my mouth but blood was running from my lips and chin and dripping onto my neck and chest. I'd never seen so much blood. I threw the toothbrush in the sink and grabbed a towel to try to stem the flow of blood. But in seconds the towel was a soaking bloody mess.

I ran to the bathroom door petrified. "Mum!" I cried, spitting blood. I caught a glimpse of my face in the landing mirror. It looked like something you might see in a butcher's shop. How could this be happening? All I'd done was brush my teeth just as I did every night. "Mum!" I cried again. There was so much blood in my mouth that I started to choke. My throat was full of it.

When my mum saw me she raised her hands and gasped. "Marvin! Marvin, what have you done?" Her face was white with fear.
"I was just brushing my teeth, Mum, that's all," I spluttered, blood spilling from my mouth.
She grabbed my arm and led me back into the bathroom. She turned on the tap and told me to rinse my mouth. I bent over the sink and watched it run pink with blood and water.

Then my mum screamed. I turned to look at her. She was holding the toothpaste tube, her eyes wide with horror. And then I realized why. My heart stopped as I stared at the tube. It wasn't toothpaste. "DANGER", it read in big capital letters. "HIGHLY TOXIC".

Then I fainted.

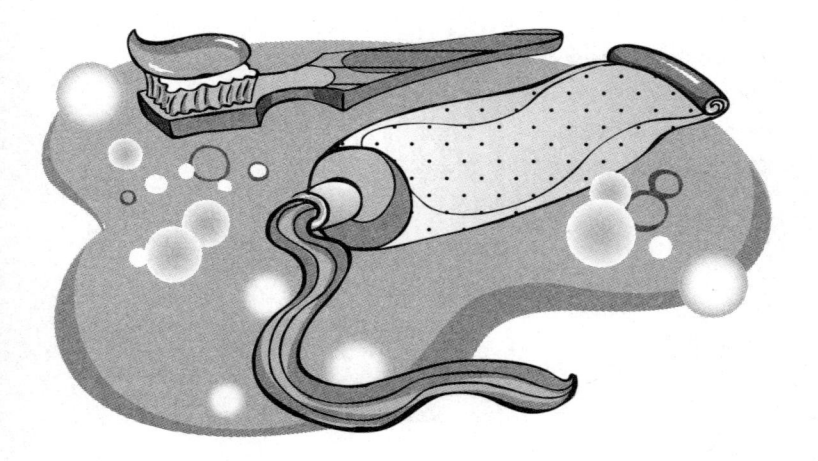

My Diary

My diary is my best friend,
my confidant with whom I share my deepest thoughts.
I tell him everything without fear that anyone else will hear.
Who else can I tell of my loves, my woes,
what I really feel about my friends and foes
and how sometimes I cannot tell the one from the other?
Only my discreet, inanimate brother.

Only my dumb inhuman brother
knows the secrets I wish I could share with some other.
The sound of laughter, the thrill of a hand's touch
in discussing those matters that mean so much –
these I lack, while, unheard by another's ear, my inked
  words curdle here.
My deepest thoughts interred within this gloomy cell.
My diary is my worst enemy.

Tommy-All-Alone

High up on the hill,
overlooking the lea,
stands Tommy-All-Alone,
the old oak tree.

In his bare branches
no birds nest or fly;
the only song you'll hear there
is the wild wind's cry.

No squirrels scamper,
no rabbits hop or run,
Tommy stands all alone
in rain and in sun.

His leaves are blighted,
his acorns drops like tears.
No one's come to gather them
for years and years and years.

Tommy's all alone,
and so it'll always be,
shunned for the souls who swung from him,
the hangman's tree.

The Science Lesson

We were all scared of our head teacher.
He could do stern like no one else
I've ever known before or since.
Just his glare could cause you to tremble;
a simple purse of his lips made you feel
much smaller than you already were;
his face and voice were as awful
as the ruler, the plimsoll, the cane,
which he used with sparing yet ruthless efficiency.
Even the teachers were scared of him.
You could see it in their eyes
when he poked his head around the classroom door
and asked if he might "have a word".

And yet, though we feared him,
we loved him.

We loved the magical stories he told us;
we loved the wild sports he invented;
but most of all, we loved his science lessons.

They were always unexpected.
We'd be *expecting* an afternoon of maths perhaps or spelling,
when he'd enter the classroom
to the sudden hush that invariably met his appearance,
carrying a sturdy wooden box
that brought a spontaneous, unified outbreath
  of excitement,
for we knew what wonders it contained.

He put the box on the table with a dangerous smile
and paused a moment before opening the lid
to reveal an array of chunky glass pyramids,
each as impressive in our eyes as any old Pharaoh's tomb.
We were overcome with awe and anticipation –
none more so than me.

Though at first bewildered why these treasures
were called "prisons" (when prisons were places
for armed robbers, thieves and murderers),
it soon became as clear as the objects themselves:
they were prisons of light,
enticing it in and holding it,
turning it to captive rainbows
that dazzled and delighted us
with their iridescent magic, holding us in thrall
for much longer than the glorious half an hour of
  our lesson.

It hardly mattered that when I went to secondary school
these "prisons" became "prisms" and I learnt
a proper science lesson about refraction, light and colour,
for my old head teacher with his box of wonders
had taught me a more enduring lesson,
which had very little to do with science,
and everything to do with poetry.

We Writers

We writers savour words,
the taste and crunch of them
on our teeth and our tongue;

We long for inspiration,
we watch jugglers tossing up letters
on the seashore and we gather up the shells;

We are greedy for images and metaphors,
we want to be the mother of our fathers
and make jam through the muslin
of our great grandmother's wedding veil;

We like heights and other dangers,
we want to peer down on the world
from a narrow ledge on the one hundred and sixty-third
floor of the Burj Khalifa;

We want to ride dragons,
we want to milk lions,
we once saw an egg blush but we did not eat it;

We want to become the offal of a cow,
a rusty nail hammered in crucifixion,
grow tulips in our mulched hearts;

We want to live in your eyes,
walk in your shoes,
eat marshmallows with gravy;

We writers want to rule the world with a uniball pen,
we want the stars to tell our stories,
we want you to believe every word
we didn't say.

Idiot Acrostic

I
Dance and sing
In the morning, at night
Over and over, hour after hour
Time means nothing to me.

Standing on Ceremony

"To stand on ceremony – to insist on behaving formally"
Chambers English Dictionary

Don't stand on Ceremony; he won't like it.
He'll stab you viciously with his medals.
He'll whip you soundly with his golden chain.
Your bones will snap beneath his sceptre,
your head shatter from the blows of his silver-tipped cane.
He'll gouge out your eyes with his white-gloved fingers.
He'll throttle you with his silk bow tie.
His shiny black boots will stamp and trample you.
His sword will slice you till your blood runs dry.
He'll bring the weight of the state down on you.
He'll crush you with his solemn vows.
His pomp will squeeze the very breath from you.
He'll nut and butt you as he takes his bows,
then bury you beneath his herd of sacred cows.
So don't stand on Ceremony; he won't like it.

Three Library Acrostics

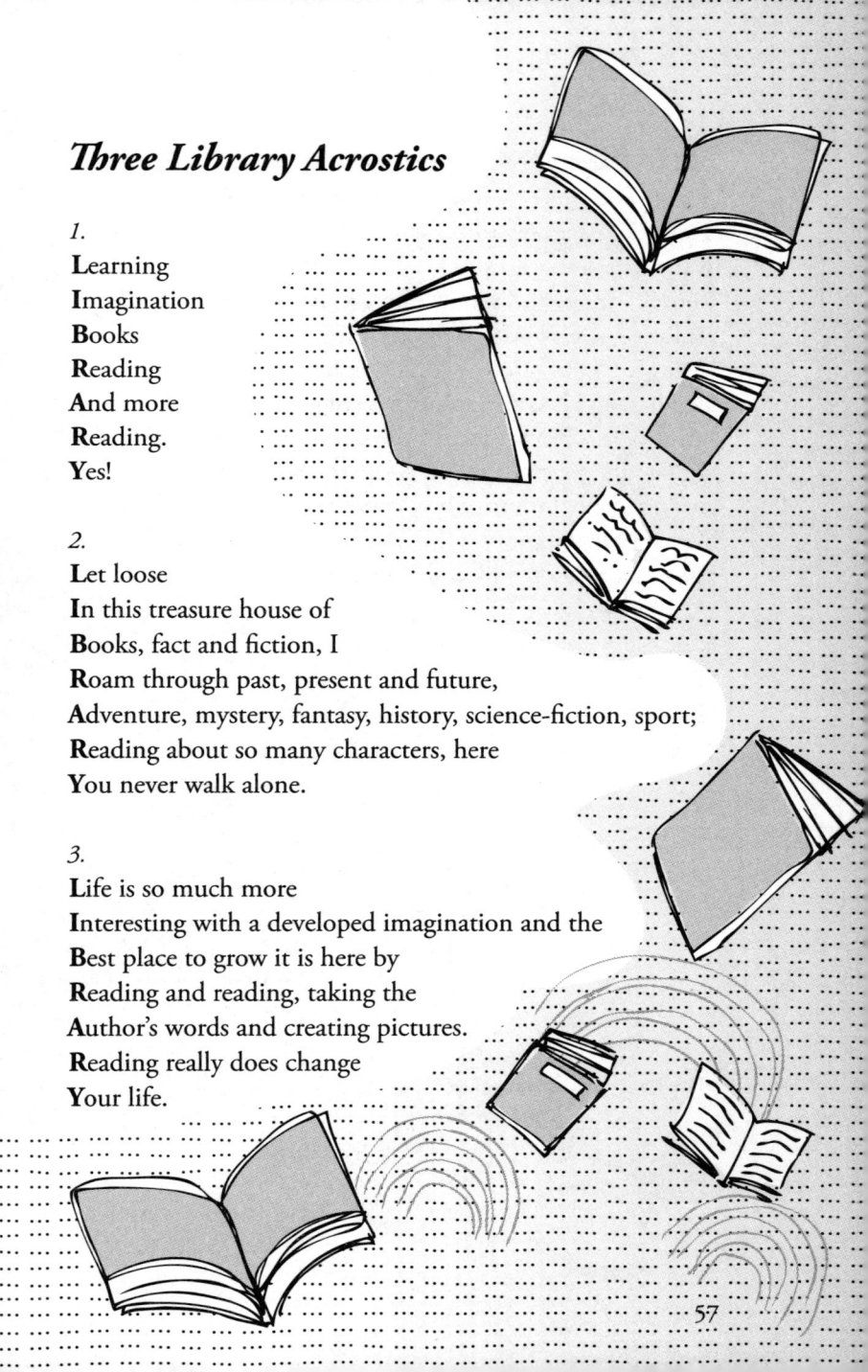

1.
Learning
Imagination
Books
Reading
And more
Reading.
Yes!

2.
Let loose
In this treasure house of
Books, fact and fiction, I
Roam through past, present and future,
Adventure, mystery, fantasy, history, science-fiction, sport;
Reading about so many characters, here
You never walk alone.

3.
Life is so much more
Interesting with a developed imagination and the
Best place to grow it is here by
Reading and reading, taking the
Author's words and creating pictures.
Reading really does change
Your life.

Time Flies

"Time flies," said my mum as she threw the alarm clock out of the window.
"Mum!" I shouted. I jumped up and ran after the clock but I couldn't get it. It was just too fast.

All day long I was chasing Time, but I couldn't catch it. I was always behind. I missed the bus, I was late for school, I was late for registration, I was late for every lesson. When I got to the lunchroom, all the food had been eaten. When I ran into the playground, the bell rang for the end of play. Time flew and I plodded along in its wake.

There weren't enough minutes in the day, it seemed, for me to do what I had to do.
"Time stands still for no man," said my teacher when I complained that I hadn't had enough time to complete my comprehension test.
"No, time flies," I sighed.
"Or, as the Ancient Romans would have put it, 'tempus fugit'," said my teacher.
Oh no, I thought, it's bad enough time flying in English, without it flying in Latin as well!

I wanted Time to slow down and rest its busy hands for a while. I wanted time to be my friend. But Time ran away, it sped like an arrow. Time was my enemy – and all because my mum threw the alarm clock out of the window.
It wasn't fair.

Who said Time flies when you're having fun?

Pink
(a poem in two attitudes)

Pink, pink, I love pink!
Pink is the bestest colour, I think.
My pyjamas are pink, my duvet is pink,
My wallpaper's pink, my ceiling is pink,
My coat is pink, my shoes are pink,
My hoody is pink, my knickers are pink,
My lips are pink, my cheeks are pink,
My tongue is pink, my lunch is pink.
Pink, pink, I love pink!

Pink, pink, I hate pink!
Pink is the worstest colour, it stinks!
Pink is fluffy, pink is yucky,
Pink is vomity, pink is vile,
Pink is disgusting, an abomination,
Pink is the colour of a baboon's bum,
Pink is for girls, pink is for babies,
Pink is my idea of hell.
Pink, pink, I hate pink!

African Animal Conundrum

Is a Zebra white and black or is it black and white?
Do hyenas laugh in humour or do they laugh in spite?
When an elephant flaps his ears is he wishing he could fly,
A giant jumbo soaring in the African sky?

Would an impala impale ya if he had a rhino's horn?
Would a cheetah cheat ya, a lion lie on your lawn?
Would a giraffe stick out its neck to save an
  endangered friend?
Does a croc's snappy patter send buffalos round the bend?

Would a leopard like to change his spots?
Does a hippopotamus carry hippo pots?
Is a jackal a jack of all trades or none?
Who knows? It's an African animal conundrum!

The Dog Who Cried "Custard!"

Once, well, no, quite a few times actually, there was a dog who cried, "Custard!"
He'd cry it at night and he'd cry it by day. Sometimes he even cried it in his sleep.
"Custard! Custard! Custard!"

It was very annoying for his neighbours. There they were all tucked up in bed and ready for sleep, when, "Custard! Custard! Custard!"
Or maybe they were in the garden, enjoying a few moments peace in the sunshine, when, "Custard! Custard! Custard!"
That dog was at his tricks again. What a nuisance he was!
"Custard! Custard! Custard!" he'd cry and, what made it even more annoying, was that there was no sign at all of the stuff. No one in that village had seen any custard for years and years. Most of the villagers didn't even know what custard was.
"Custard is a kind of insect with wings and a trunk," one suggested.
"No, no," said another. "Custard is a farming tool used for harvesting peanuts."
"Don't be silly," said a third. "Custard is a hooded cloak worn on Sundays by mountain pixies."
"Custard! Custard! Custard!" cried the dog.

After a while, as is the way with these things, the villagers got used to the dog's cries and no one paid them any attention. They became as ordinary a part of the soundscape as a pigeon cooing or a door slamming.

Then one day, something terrible happened. A flood of hot custard came down from the mountain and swept through that village like lava, destroying everything and everyone in its path. Nothing was saved.

And do you know what? That dog never said a thing.

And the moral of this fable is (and it's very important so listen carefully): *Don't mess with custard!*

Three Wishes

Once upon a time there was an enormous hippopotamus, who lived in a river. He was a prince among hippos and had a lovely life splashing about in the water. But he wasn't a happy hippo. He saw the humans sailing by in their boats and he thought that he should be a prince among *them*. He was sure that a witch had put a curse on him and turned him into a hippo when really he was a handsome human prince.

Now, as often happens in tales like this, one day a witch passed by. The hippo called out to her and told her what he thought about the being a prince business. She laughed and laughed – well, cackled actually, as witches do.
"I've heard of princes being turned into frogs," she grinned, "but never hippos. What you need is a beautiful princess to kiss you."
"Oh," sighed the hippo.
"Look," said the witch, "as you've entertained me, I'll grant you three wishes."
"Thank you," said the hippo – and he wished for a beautiful princess.

His wish was granted. Smack! The princess kissed him and – hey presto! – nothing happened. He was still a hippo. So he made his second wish.

"I wish I was a handsome prince," he wished and – hey presto! – he was! He really was.
"Now we can get married," he said to the beautiful princess. But she shook her head. "I don't want to get married," she said. "I want to be a pop star. Anyway, you smell funny." And off she went.

The enormous hippopotamus prince was as miserable as mud. He saw all his friends splashing about in the river and having a fine old time. I wish I were a hippo again, he thought and – hey presto! – he was.

And he lived hippoly ever after.

Trick or Treat

Trick or treat! Trick or treat!
Shout it out to whoever you meet.
In every house, in every street.
Trick or treat!

Beware of Barry the axeman,
(that's him in the blood-stained top).
Make sure he gets what he asks for.
or you'll be for the chop.

There's wicked witch Pradeepa,
and Bob, her wicked witch's dog.
Fill up her cauldron with candy,
or she'll turn you into a frog.

Trick or treat! Trick or treat!
Shout it out to whoever you meet.
In every house, in every street.
Trick or treat!

Marvin's the one in the devil mask,
the skull-faced ghoul is Mel.
Send them away with chocolate,
or *they'll* send you to Hell.

Meet Frank, that's Frankenstein's monster
and Mummy who's nobody's mum.
Offer them mints to munch on,
or they'll chew you up like gum.

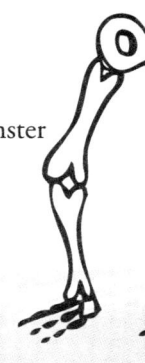

Trick or treat! Trick or treat!
Shout it out to whoever you meet.
In every house, in every street.
Trick or treat!

There's Vincent (he's a vampire)
and his toothy sidekick Bud.
Give them something sweet to suck on,
or they will suck your blood.

So whatever comes a-knocking,
be it ghost or ghoul or beast
Give them confectionery in abundance,
or you'll be their hallowe'en feast!

Trick or treat! Trick or treat!
Shout it out to whoever you meet.
In every house, in every street.
TRICK OR TREAT!

The Moment After

Every picture tells a story they say,
but what about the one that got away –
the moment after, not captured in black and white,
when the smile slipped, the bird took flight?
Take this photo, for example, the quaint still
of me as a child and Granny and Granny's dog Bill
in the square, coming home from the shop that day.
Granny's sitting on the bench that marked halfway,
holding the paper she'd bought, trailing a string
that's attached to Bill, sitting up beside her like a king,
taking the eye's focus where he perches facing me
Who am standing apart a little, leaning on a tree,
while our neighbour, Mrs Luckett, dressed up in black
stands over Granny chatting and Granny chats back,
and at the bench's end, balancing Bill,
is a small silvery bucket of galvanised steel,
which doesn't appear to belong to anyone there
and is barely visible to the casual stare.
This then is the photo before me now –
a good photo, interesting, alluring somehow,
remarkable enough to provoke smiles, even laughter,
but nothing to what happened the moment after,
when Bill looked at the tethering string and said,
"Sometimes I wish I were a cat instead"
and with a gasp and a gurgle, poor Mrs Luckett
dropped like a stone and kicked the bucket.

Valentine's Poem

Violets are red,
Roses are blue,
A cow kissed a bull
And said, "I love moo!"

Catastrophe

The way she swings from the curtains like a pirate on a rope
and crashes face-first into the window;
the way she stands up like a meerkat, scrabbling at the glass
to catch a spinning spider on the other side;
the way she climbs into the shopping bags the instant
  they're empty;
the way she nuzzles and suckles her furry blanket
with a rapturous purring;
the way she rolls on her side with her ginger tum exposed
and stretches out a languid paw;
the way she sharpens her claws on the brand new sofa;
the way she digs up potted plants for fun and nibbles
  at flowers;
the way she plays football with a marble, dribbling
  it cleverly
between her paws;

the way she stalks my bare toes beneath the duvet
and pushes her nose into my face to wake me;
the way she pounces on my boot and burrows in
to find the ball of paper I dropped there;
the way she leaps up on to the narrow sill of the bath
and falls in;
the way she chases sticks and retrieves them like a puppy;
the way her eyes open suddenly in a wild wide stare;
the way she scuttles after squirrels and squares up
to mogs twice her size;
the way she refuses to open the cat flap;
the way she types a path across the computer keyboard
and tries to catch tennis balls on the tv screen;
the way she eats jigsaw puzzle pieces;
the way she steals the cream;
the way she is what she is.
My cat's a catastrophe and I love her!

Have You Ever Contemplated?

Have you (not now for instance
but in this space of time)
contemplated the end of you this summer next
or after, but not for ever,
have you?

Have you (perhaps awake or
down below sleep)
contemplated the edge of this one into
the next, or onward further,
have you?

Have you (here now where we're at)
wished you did not have to
contemplate either me or you until death's end,
but that you knew,
have you?

The Dream

I was walking to school one morning when a man came up to me carrying a clipboard. He said he was conducting a survey and did I mind taking a few minutes to answer some questions. "OK," I said. "Thanks," he said, turning into my mum. "Have you got your swimming kit?" she asked. "Yes," I replied. "Have you met the Prime Minister?" she asked. "No," I said, because he only came to school on Tuesdays and Thursdays. "Look out, mum!" I cried. We were in the jungle now and a huge tiger was right behind her. But it was too late: the tiger ate her. "That was nice," purred the tiger, "only a little less mustard next time if you please" and he went back into the rabbit hutch that I had built for him in the garden. I carried on walking to school, only it was dark now and the moon was out and I was worried that I'd left my science homework behind in the cat. I was late and I wanted to run but I couldn't control my legs and the fish fins I'd grown weren't helping. "Is this the way to school?" I asked the old man who'd been there all along, though I hadn't seen him. He said something in French, which I understood perfectly. I went down a long winding road past some yellow trees and suddenly I was back home again, lying in bed. And then I woke up … and it was all true!

If I Won the Lottery

If I won the lottery it would be a huge surprise because I've never bought a ticket. Well, I am only ten years old and you have to be over sixteen, I think, to buy a lottery ticket. But let's say that I found the ticket in the street and it turned out to be the winning ticket and I was allowed to have the prize, even though I am only ten. Let's pretend that. Let's pretend too that it was a rollover that week and the amount of money I won was twenty million pounds. Twenty million pounds, imagine that!

What would I do with it all? Well, for a start I would buy ten Curly Wurlies from the sweetshop at the end of my road, because I like Curly Wurlies a lot. Curly Wurlies cost 40p each, so that would come to £4. That would leave me £19, 999,996.

I could buy myself a mansion – or two perhaps, one for me and one for my family. I wouldn't want to move though because I would miss my friends. I could buy a Ferrari, only that would be a waste because I couldn't drive it as I am only ten. I could buy a very good new bike, but bikes, especially nice new ones, usually get stolen where I live. I could buy a really expensive mobile phone, but then I might get mugged.

To be honest, I'm not sure I'd like to win the lottery. I think I'm happy as I am – except I would like the Curly Wurlies. So let's say I won the lottery but it wasn't a rollover and lots of other people won it that week and the amount that I won was £4. Just £4.

Yes, I'd be happy with that.

Moving

Goodbye, old house,
goodbye, old street,
no more will your pavement
feel the tap of my feet.
I wonder what sort of people I'll meet
in my new house.

Goodbye, old house,
goodbye, old park,
no more will your gardens
hear my little dog's bark,
it feels like I'm disappearing into the dark
In my new house.

Goodbye, old house,
goodbye, old school,
no more in your playground
will I throw or kick a ball,
Will I ever make any new friends at all
in my new house?

Goodbye, old house,
goodbye, old room,
no more in your mirror
will I play guitar broom.
Am I making a new start or going to my doom?
in my new house.

Goodbye, old house,
goodbye, farewell,
all the times we shared
I remember them so well.
But now I'm moving, there are new tales to tell
in my new house.

Noughts and Crosses

If life were a sequence of noughts and crosses,
Where noughts denoted regrets and losses,
And crosses marked the spots of our joy and success,
Your name would appear as xxx.

Home At Last

The church clock chimed: dong, dong, dong…
She was running out of time. Hurrying through the darkness she could hear shouting behind her – and the barking of dogs. She shivered. They were on her trail. If she didn't reach home soon, they would surely catch her – and then what? The dogs would tear her to pieces.

An owl swooped and screeched just above her. It was oddly reassuring, almost comforting. Perhaps there was still time if she gathered all her strength and energy and willed herself on…

She sprinted as quickly as she could but the shouts and barking were getting closer. A howl of excitement pierced the air and made her blood run cold. They thought they had her.

Her breathing was ragged and raspy. She felt faint and light-headed as though she lacked sustenance, but she had had plenty tonight.

The baying of hound and human seemed so close it was as if it was all around her, when finally she saw the graveyard wall. With a supernatural act of determination she drove herself on, slithered up and over the old stone wall and staggered across the soft mossy turf.

The first drops of sunlight were speckling the yew tree as she reached her destination. She glanced at the headstone – Mary Travers 1747 – 1764 RIP – and the open grave beneath it.

As the cemetery gates crashed open, she was already halfway inside the grave. She lay down and pulled the marble slab across, until she was in total darkness. She wiped the blood from her fangs and smiled. She was safe. She was home at last.

Crossing the Bridge

We stand at the edge of the bridge,
One world in front, one world behind,
We are ready to cross but first glance back
To where the paths of our school days unwind.

We see laughter and companionship,
Times of triumph and of tears too,
Lessons well learnt, games played hard but fair,
Teachers and friends who helped us through.

We all have our special memories,
The shows we performed, the meals we ate,
Sports days, school trips, festive parties,
We reflect and remember as we stand and wait.

But now it is time to say farewell,
To step onto the bridge, tread our new way,
With a wave we cross, the land ahead shines bright,
Yet we will never forget this, our leaving day.